This book belongs to:

Yareli Fernandez Muñoz

Ismael Fernandez Muñoz

Maria Fernandez (?)

Retold by Gaby Goldsack
Illustrated by Ruth Galloway
Designed by Jester Designs

Language consultant: Betty Root

ISBN 1-40543-889-4

This is a P³ Book
This edition published in 2004

P³
Queen Street House
4 Queen Street
Bath BA1 1HE, UK

p^3

Goldilocks
and the
Three Bears

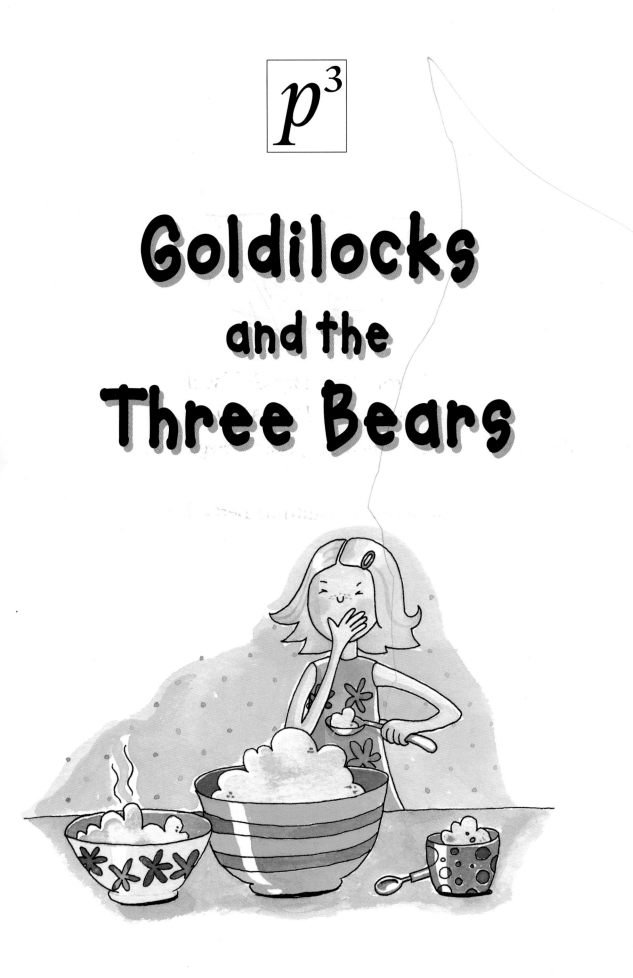

Helping Your Child Read

Learning to read is an exciting challenge for most children. From a very early age, sharing story books with children, talking about the pictures, and guessing what might happen next are all very important parts of the reading experience.

Sharing Reading

Set aside a regular quiet time to share reading with younger children, or to be available to encourage older children as they develop into independent readers.

First Readers are intended to encourage and support the early stages of learning to read. They present well-loved tales that children will enjoy hearing again and again. Familiarity helps children identify some of the words and phrases.

When you feel your child is ready to move ahead, encourage him or her to join in so that you read the story aloud together. Always pause to talk about the pictures. The easy-to-read speech bubbles in **First Readers** provide an excellent "joining-in" activity. The bright, clear illustrations and matching text will help children to understand the story.

Building Confidence

In time, children will want to read *to* you. When this happens, be patient and give continual praise. They may not read all the words correctly, but children's substitutions are often very good guesses.

The repetition in each book is especially helpful for building confidence. If your child cannot read a particular word, go back to the beginning of the sentence and read it together so the meaning is not lost. Most importantly, do not continue if your child is tired or just needs a change.

Reading Alone

The next step is for your child to read alone. Try to be available to give help and support. Remember to give lots of encouragement and praise.

Together with other simple stories, **First Readers** will help ensure reading is an enjoyable and rewarding experience for children.

Once upon a time there were three
bears. They lived in a little house
in the big woods.

There was great big Daddy Bear.

Then there was middle-sized Mommy Bear.

And there was tiny little Baby Bear.

One day, Mommy Bear made porridge
She put some in a great big bowl.

She put some in a middle-sized bowl.
And she put some in a tiny little bowl.

The porridge was too hot to eat.
The three bears went for a walk
while it cooled down.

Not far away, a little girl was also walking in the big woods. The little girl had golden hair. She was called Goldilocks.

Is anyone home?

Soon Goldilocks found the house of the three bears. The door was wide open.

Goldilocks walked right into the house.
She saw the bowls of porridge. She
tasted some from the great big bowl.
It was too salty.

She tasted some from the middle-sized
bowl. It was too sweet.

She tasted some from the tiny little bowl. It was just right. Goldilocks ate it all up!

15

Then Goldilocks saw three chairs.
She sat in the great big chair. It was
too high.

She sat in the middle-sized chair. It was
too low.

She sat in the tiny little chair. It was just right.

Crack! Oh no, it wasn't! Goldilocks was too heavy. The tiny little chair broke into pieces.

Next Goldilocks went upstairs.

She lay on the great big bed. It was too hard.

Too hard!

She lay on the middle-sized bed. It was too soft.

She lay on the tiny little bed. It was just right, and Goldilocks fell asleep.

Soon the three bears came home.

"Who's been eating my porridge?"
asked Daddy Bear in a great big voice.

"Who's been eating my porridge?" asked
Mommy Bear in a middle-sized voice.

"Who's been eating my porridge, and eaten it all up?" asked Baby Bear in a tiny little voice.

21

Then the three bears saw their chairs.

"Who's been sitting in my chair?" said
Daddy Bear in a great big voice.

Oh no!

"Who's been sitting in my chair?" said
Mommy Bear in a middle-sized voice.

"Who's been sitting in my chair and broken it?" said Baby Bear in a tiny little voice.

Then the three bears went upstairs.

"Who's been sleeping in my bed?" asked Daddy Bear in a great big voice.

"Who's been sleeping in my bed?" asked Mommy Bear in a middle-sized voice.

"Who's three bears did not see Goldilocks Baby Beagain. she's still he.

27

Read and Say

How many of these words can you say? The pictures will help you. Look back in your book and see if you can find the words in the story.

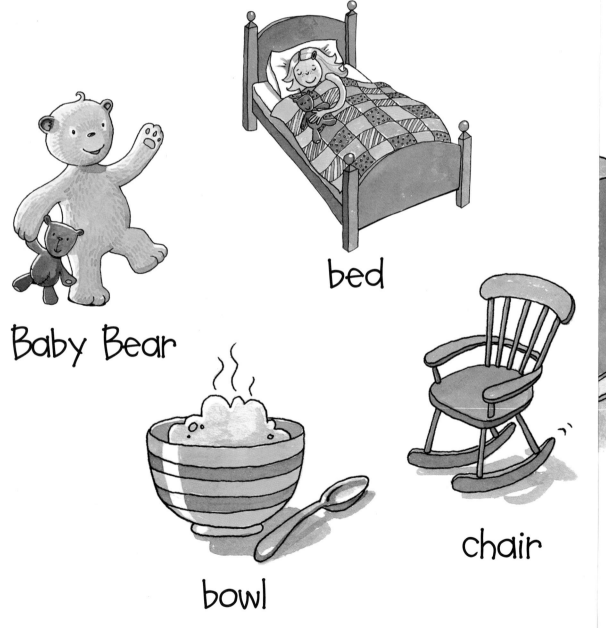

Baby Bear

bed

bowl

chair

Daddy Bear

door

Goldilocks

house

Mommy Bear

woods

Titles in this series:

we v